WALT DISNEY'S Bambi

Illustrated by the Disney Storybook Artists
Bambi from the story by Felix Salten
Adapted by Kate Hannigan

© Disney Enterprises, Inc.
Visit our Web site at www.disneybooks.com

Published by
Louis Weber, C.E.O.
Publications International, Ltd.
7373 North Cicero Avenue
Lincolnwood, Illinois 60712

www.pilbooks.com

Manufactured in China.

8 7 6 5 4 3 2 1

ISBN: 0-7853-9540-7

On a bright spring morning deep in the woods, a little rabbit called Thumper ran to Friend Owl's tree with some exciting news. He called to the old bird to wake up. "The new prince is born!" he shouted.

All the animals of the forest gathered around to meet the newborn. They asked his mother what she was going to name him. "Bambi," she said.

Bambi's mother introduced him to the animals. Mrs. Quail and her chicks hurried by and said hello. Bambi greeted Mrs. Opossum and her babies as they hung upside down from a tree. And a little mole poked his head out of the ground and welcomed him.

Bambi also met Thumper. The little rabbit laughed when Bambi stumbled on his long legs. He said Bambi didn't walk very well.

Mrs. Rabbit scolded Thumper. "What did your father tell you this morning?" she asked.

Thumper knew he was in trouble. "If you can't say something nice," he said, "don't say nothin' at all."

Bambi learned to walk and run. Before long, he pranced off to play in the woods with Thumper and the other rabbits. They tried to teach Bambi how to talk.

The rabbits called out "birds" when a family of bluebirds flew by. Bambi tried and tried. "Birds!" he finally shouted. The rabbits cheered.

When a butterfly landed on Bambi's tail, he called that a bird, too. Thumper laughed and told Bambi it was a butterfly. Then Bambi saw a flower. He called that a butterfly, too.

Thumper laughed even harder. He told Bambi it was a flower, not a butterfly.

Bambi poked his nose in the petals. Suddenly the flower started to move! A skunk peered up at Bambi. Bambi called the skunk a flower. Thumper laughed so hard that he fell over. His leg started to thump! "That's not a flower! He's a little..."

"That's all right," interrupted the skunk. "He can call me Flower if he wants to!"

The three animals became best friends.

One sunny afternoon, Bambi's mother took him to a
new place on the other side of the forest. She called it the
meadow. Bambi couldn't wait to see it!

When they finally reached the open field, Bambi started
to bolt ahead. His mother jumped in front of him and
blocked the way. She warned Bambi that he should never
rush out into the meadow. There were no trees or bushes
there to protect them.

Bambi's mother walked slowly out of the woods. She
turned her head from side to side and looked for danger.
Finally she called Bambi's name. It was safe.

Bambi ran through the green grass and jumped over streams! It felt wonderful to be so free! He saw frogs and ducks and all kinds of new things. And for the first time, Bambi saw other deer.

"That's little Faline," his mother said. Bambi was afraid of the young deer, but Faline wasn't shy. She gave Bambi a kiss on his cheek! Soon the two began to play.

Bambi and Faline chased and leaped through the grass. Suddenly everyone stopped and stood perfectly still. Bambi didn't know what was happening!

Then he saw him. A mighty buck appeared in the clearing. He towered above the other deer. Bambi thought his antlers seemed to reach the sky.

As the buck walked past Bambi, he looked deep into the young deer's eyes. Bambi was amazed and told his mother about it. She said all the animals in the forest respected the mighty buck. "He's very brave and very wise," she explained. "That's why he's known as the Great Prince of the Forest."

Just then, birds in the nearby trees flew into the air. Their cries of warning shattered the quiet of the meadow. The deer began to run in panic.

Bambi heard the sounds of hunting dogs. He looked around for his mother as the other deer ran past him. He couldn't find her. In a flash, the Great Prince ran to Bambi's side and led him to safety.

Later that evening, when Bambi was nestled safely in
the thicket with his mother, he asked her why the deer had
run away. She told him Man was in the forest. Bambi
didn't quite understand, but he was afraid.

Slowly the seasons passed. Summer turned to fall, and
fall to winter. One morning Bambi woke up and saw
something white and cold covering the ground. It was
snow! It seemed to cover the whole forest, Bambi thought.

Bambi left deep tracks as he walked through the crunchy snow. Soon he found his friend Thumper gliding on the frozen pond. "It's all right," Thumper assured him, "the water's stiff!"

Bambi took a few steps onto the ice and began to slip and slide! He couldn't keep his long legs where they belonged. Thumper tried to teach Bambi how to skate on the ice, but it was no use. They crashed right into a tall snowdrift and uncovered Flower. Their friend was sleeping through the winter!

Winter seemed to last forever. Bambi and his mother searched everywhere for food. Finally, on a cold afternoon, they saw the first shoots of green grass poking up through the snow. It was a sign that spring was coming!

When the snows finally melted, it was time for Bambi to be on his own. Springtime brought changes to the forest, and to the animals, too. Bambi had grown the antlers of a young buck, and his legs had become more sturdy.

Thumper and Flower looked different, too. Friend Owl couldn't get over how much they had changed over the long winter. As the friends greeted one another, they noticed the birds circling and dipping strangely above them. Bambi asked Owl what the matter was.

"Don't you know? They're twitterpated!" said Friend Owl. "Nearly everybody gets twitterpated in the springtime."

Bambi, Thumper, and Flower didn't understand. Owl explained that twitterpated meant they'd fallen in love. It sounded just awful, the friends thought.

Bambi, Thumper, and Flower watched the swooping, swooning birds and shook their heads. Twitterpated? Bah! Thumper said it wasn't going to happen to him. Bambi and Flower agreed, saying they would never let themselves become twitterpated either.

As the three friends marched off, Flower caught the eye of a beautiful girl skunk. She smiled and waved at him. He waved back. The little girl skunk walked up to Flower and kissed him. That's all it took. Flower was twitterpated!

Bambi and Thumper were shocked! They walked on into the forest, and soon they came across a pretty young rabbit. She gave Thumper a look. Thumper froze in his tracks. Then she fluttered her eyelashes. Thumper began to thump his leg! Suddenly he was twitterpated, too!

That left only Bambi. He couldn't believe his friends. "Twitterpated! What were they thinking?" Bambi wondered. He stopped at a stream for a drink of water. "Hello, Bambi," said a gentle voice. Bambi looked up. It was Faline!

Bambi was surprised to see his old friend. He stumbled backward and fell right into the water with a splash! As he scrambled to his feet, his antlers got caught in a tree branch. He felt ridiculous!

Bambi was embarrassed and excited at the same time. He thought Faline was beautiful. But when he tried to speak, no sounds came out of his mouth! Faline stepped closer to Bambi and placed a kiss right on his cheek, just as she'd done when they were younger!

That did it — Bambi was twitterpated!

But he wasn't the only one who had fallen in love with Faline. A buck called Ronno was very jealous and challenged Bambi to a fight. They charged each other, butting heads in a fierce battle. The bucks locked antlers and wrestled wildly up and down the rocks. Finally, Bambi won the fight.

After that, Bambi and Faline were always together.

Later that spring, Bambi awoke to a strange smell in the forest. It was smoke! He had to warn the other animals. There was no time to waste!

Bambi ran to the thicket to tell Faline, but she was gone. Hunting dogs had cornered her on a rocky cliff. Bambi fought the dogs, and Faline escaped into the woods.

Bambi got away, too. But he was exhausted from the fight. He collapsed on the smoky forest floor, too tired to run another step. Just in time, the Great Prince of the Forest appeared. The Great Prince of the Forest told Bambi that he was his father.

"You must get up, Bambi," the Great Prince said. Bambi rose to his feet and ran with the Great Prince through the forest. The fire raged behind them as they jumped into a river. They swam to safety on a nearby island. "Son, you are brave," said the Great Prince. "I am very proud of you."

"Bambi, is it you?" called Faline anxiously. She was waiting there with the other forest animals. They all had escaped the terrible fire.

Eventually the animals returned to the woods. On a bright spring morning, Thumper and his babies were back at Friend Owl's tree with exciting news. Faline had given birth to twins! Now Bambi was a proud father, too.

Bambi stood on the nearby rocks with the Great Prince.

"It's time for me to leave," the Great Prince said. "It is your turn to rule the forest." Bambi watched his father disappear into the woods. He knew he would teach his children to be brave and wise, just as the Great Prince had taught him.